ALIEN
SEARCH SQUAD

Written by
Jenny Moore

Illustrated by
Jared MacPherson

Chapter 1
Alien Alert!

Agent Will Seak held up the flashing alien locator.

"Non-Earth life force detected in Devon!" he told the team.

"Excellent," said his partner, Agent Hope Fynde. "Let's go! You too, Trace," she added, tugging at her dog's lead. "It's time to sniff out some more aliens."

The Alien Search Squad changed into their protective suits and raced to the van.

Agent Seak typed the co-ordinates from the locator into the satnav. "It looks like we're heading to the coast. Maybe we can have a paddle in the sea afterwards," he joked.

Everyone laughed, except for Agent Max Peeve.

The search squad put on their infra-red googles and slipped out of the van into the shadows. The night was cold, the salty sea breeze whipping at their cheeks.

"Good boy," said Agent Fynde, patting Trace's head. "He's got the scent already," she told the others. "This way. Follow me!"

She led the team of alien hunters up a narrow street to a small seaside cottage with shells around the windows.

"This is it," she said. "This is where the aliens are."

Agent Peeve frowned. "How can you tell? Why isn't Trace barking?"

Agent Fynde rolled her eyes. "Because he's a stealth sniffer dog," she whispered. "We don't want the aliens to hear us coming. You'll just have to trust me. I know my dog and I know this is the right place."

"Good work," said Seak. "Have you got the laser lock-breaker, Peeve?"

Peeve nodded, pulling a glowing green key out of his pocket and pressing it to the lock. "Stand back, everyone! I'm in charge of gadgets."

The team stepped back, shielding their eyes against a sudden burst of white light.

"That should do it." Peeve pushed at the door and it swung open.

"Nice work," said Fynde. "Alright then, Trace. Show us where the aliens are." She tugged on his lead and Trace led the Search Squad up some creaky stairs...

Creeeak!

...along a narrow landing with squeaky floorboards...

Squeeeeak!

...and came to a stop outside a closed bedroom door.

"Okay, Search Squad," said Fynde. "Ready to catch some aliens?"

The others nodded.

"On the count of three," said Seak.

ONE...
TWO...
THREE!

The old lady's face turned white.

The old man's face turned red.

Then both their faces turned green as they slipped off their human shape and transformed back into big, slimy aliens.

"Please don't blast us," begged the first alien, her five eyes blinking hard. "We're here in peace."

"We don't want any trouble," added the second alien, his stripy antennae wobbling in fear.

"Okay. Bananas down, everyone," said Seak. "Don't worry," he told the aliens. "We come in peace too. But you're trespassing on our planet, and I'm afraid we're going to have to take you in. It's for your own safety as much as ours. We can't risk the public finding out the truth about you. It's too dangerous."

The aliens nodded sadly. "That's why we've been in disguise all this time. We've watched enough of your Earth movies since we've been here to know what happens to aliens. It never ends well."

"Where are you taking us?" they asked as the search squad led them to the waiting van.

"To a secure unit on a secret island," said Seak.

"So secret it doesn't appear on any maps," Peeve piped up. "It's where S.T.O.D.G.E have their headquarters too."

"Stodge?" the first alien wrinkled her nose. "What's that?"

"It stands for Secret Technology Organisation for the Development of Gadgets and Equipment," Peeve explained. His face gleamed in the moonlight. "They make all sorts of amazing gadgets: exploding pencils, hypnotising sunglasses, smell-blocker tablets and powerful stun guns. I wonder if the guns stun aliens too? Maybe we should try them out."

Fynde shot Peeve a warning look. "S.T.O.D.G.E won't stay secret for very long if you keep telling everyone about it," she pointed out. "And no stun gun experiments, got it? We don't want intergalactic war breaking out."

Peeve stuck out his lip in a sulky pout. "Sorry," he mumbled, although he didn't sound very sorry.

Chapter 3
The Secret Island

Four hours later, the search squad van drove out of a hidden underwater tunnel onto the secret island.

"Well done on another successful mission," Seak told the team, blinking in the morning sun. "Fynde and I will finish off here. You guys go and get some rest."

"Why don't you let someone else take the prisoners for a change?" said Peeve. "I can do it," he suggested.

"Thanks for the offer but it's our job to deliver them safely," said Fynde. "This way," she told the aliens, brushing past Peeve and heading for the secret alien unit.

"We need to keep our eye on Peeve," she told Seak once they'd taken care of the aliens. "He's been acting strangely lately."

"I agree," said Seak. "Although we won't be working with him for much longer. Our search is almost over." He checked his watch. "Oops, we'd better hurry. It's almost time for our call with the prime minister. We don't want to keep her waiting."

They hurried over to Search Squad HQ and took their places in front of the big screen.

"I never get tired of this," whispered Fynde. "It still amazes me that the most important person in the land wants to talk to *us.*"

"I know," agreed Seak with a grin. "I get shivers every time!" He stopped talking as the prime minister appeared on the screen.

"Good morning, Agents Seak and Fynde," she said. "I hear you've completed another successful mission. How many aliens have you found now?"

Chapter 4
The Final Countdown

Seak and Fynde watched Agent Peeve closely over the next few days. But they both had the feeling that he was watching them closely too.

"Every time I turn round, there he is," grumbled Fynde. "He's like my shadow! I even caught him trying to see inside my locker yesterday. He's been acting strangely around Trace lately as well."

"He's probably jealous," said Seak. "I think he wants our jobs! He seems to think he'd be able to locate the aliens just as easily if we gave him the chance."

Fynde laughed. "I doubt it!" Her face grew serious again.

"Mind you, we haven't found any aliens for almost a week," she added, sounding worried. "Are you sure the locator's still working?"

"I'm sure." Seak showed her the 'searching' message on the locator's screen. "We'll just have to be patient."

But then, right on cue, the alien locator began to flash.

"At last!" cried Seak. His face flushed with excitement. "You get Trace, and I'll call the rest of the team!"

The Alien Search Squad assembled in record time.

"Non-Earth life force detected in London!" Seak told them. "Get your suits on, and let's get going!"

Everyone raced to get their protective suits on... everyone except Agent Peeve.

"Hey," said Fynde as she spotted Peeve feeding something to Trace. "What are you doing? What was that you just gave him?"

Peeve jumped, his cheeks turning red. "Oh... er... nothing. Just some dog treats. Sorry, I didn't think you'd mind."

"Well I do mind," said Fynde. "You leave Trace alone."

Well done, everyone. Let's go!

Wait, it looks like there are more aliens nearby!

Beep Beep

Fynde shook her head in amazement. "Who knew there were so many aliens hiding out in London?"

"And we still haven't found them all," said Seak. "One more to go. Not for long though... look, the locator's flashing again! I wonder what human disguise our last alien chose?"

Fynde grinned. "We'll soon find out. Trace has got the scent already. This way, everyone." She led the team to a deserted school, where a tired alien teacher had fallen asleep at his desk, his head resting on a pile of half-marked homework.

The teacher jerked awake as the squad moved into position, surrounding him.

"Help!" he cried, spotting the banana blasters. "Please don't shoot! I'll come quietly." He held up his hands and changed back into his alien form.

"Don't worry," said Fynde kindly as they led him away. "We'll take good care of you."

"Well done, team!" said Seak. "That's our last alien!"

"Really?" said Peeve, who was standing by the teacher's bin. "Hmm," he muttered. "We'll see about that."

Peeve raised his eyebrows. "Don't you think it's strange that Seak knew exactly where to find the shipwrecked alien spacecraft? *And* he knew how to use the locator."

"That doesn't prove anything," said Seak.

"But I can prove we're not aliens," said Fynde, pulling a banana out of her holster and peeling it. She took a big bite and swallowed it. "There! Could an alien do that?"

"They could if their so-called banana allergy was just a cover story. I found two banana skins in the teacher's bin last night, so I know he wasn't allergic to them. I think the bananas are a secret signal to show your alien friends that you're aliens in disguise too," he said, pointing to Seak and Fynde. "That's how they know not to fight back."

Seak and Fynde exchanged a nervous glance.

The prime minister frowned. "These are very serious accusations, Agent Peeve. Are you sure?"

Peeve nodded. "I broke into Agent Fynde's locker with the laser lock-breaker a few minutes ago and found this." He held up a strange, glowing blue stone.

Everyone gasped.

"I think this is the missing part of their spaceship," said Peeve. "And now they've found it, they've been rounding up their friends ready to fly away again. Confess everything," he demanded, "or I'll destroy your precious stone."

"No! Be careful," said Fynde. "It's not part of a spaceship, it's a mallicator egg we found in the external drive shaft!"

"A what?" repeated the prime minister.

"A mallicator egg," repeated Fynde. "They're popular pets where we come from, but they're very dangerous for humans. Agent Peeve is right. We are aliens," she admitted. "We're from a planet two-trillion light years away. Our ship got caught in a space storm and we were sucked through a powerful temporary wormhole that only appears once every ten years. It brought us here, to Earth. We've been waiting for the next wormhole to take us back home ever since!"

"We decided to split up and try out life on Earth while we were waiting," added Seak. "It's been good fun, and we really like your bananas, but we want to go home now."

Once everyone was safely on board, Seak and Fynde came back for the mallicator, who was now the size of a whale!

"Good boy," said Seak, stroking the creature's slimy back.

"You're a good boy too," said Fynde as Trace licked her leg. "I think he wants to come with us!" She turned to Peeve. "If you promise to let us go in peace, we'll call off the mallicator."

"I promise," he yelped. "Take the dog as well, that's fine!"

"I promise too," said the prime minister. "Good luck."

Seak let out a big sigh of relief as they flew towards the wormhole. "It's good to be back in our true forms at last!"

"You can turn back as well now," Fynde told the mallicator. She laughed as the creature transformed into a cute two-headed puppy, nuzzling up against his new friend, Trace. "You'd never eat anyone, would you, boy? How about a banana instead?" She pulled out an entire crate of bananas. "I thought I'd stock up for the flight home!"

The End

WHAT NEXT?

Did you enjoy this Fusion Reader? If you are looking for more, the Maverick Reading Scheme is a bright, attractive range of books with plenty of stories for everyone.

MAVERICK FUSION READERS

To view the whole Maverick Reading Scheme, visit our website at www.maverickearlyreaders.com

Or scan the QR code to view our scheme instantly!